THE LOST PRINCESS

RALESIA

MK TAYYIBAH AREEF

This book is dedicated to my mother - (L) Fatima.

Your life will remain eternal in those letters of this book.

I thanked you for all your affection and for this wonderful life.

" I MISS YOU A LOT "

" REST IN PEACE IN HEAVEN "

Contents

Preface

This book is the first book which I've written. And I started to write this story from my eighth standard. I'm very fond of barbie movies and fairy tales. And I used to read fiction novel often. One day, I thought how about writing a magic fairy tale. I got a lot of support and suggestion from my friends. And today I got to stay as an author because I had supports from them and I'll never forget them.

Don't stay back, don't get fear. Just move forward. Don't miss the opportunities as it doesn't comes to all. Everyone has a will to win but very few have the will to prepare to win. Don't hesitate. Be confident.

Acknowledgements

I'll be happy to take names of those who had helped me in making this book. They are :
1) Sm. Jidana
2) Sahibah Idrish
3) Aktari Mansam
4) Ruqqayah Mk.

After I completed this story, this was checked by Sir David Keishing, Sir Kipchen, Sir Sharif Khullakpham. Sir Sharif guided me how to write with no mistake. I am very grateful to you all.

Thank you

ONE
CAST

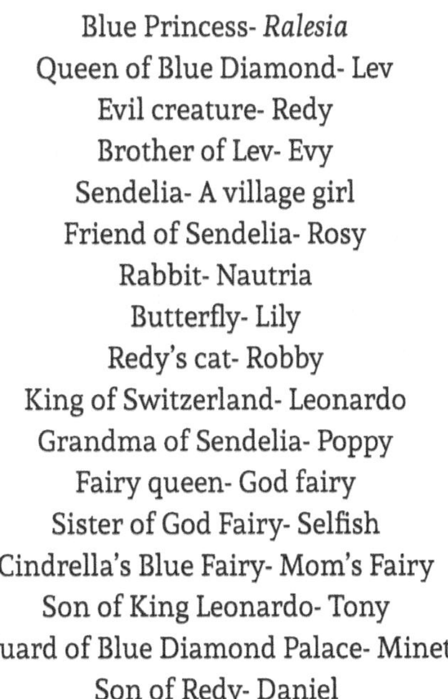

Blue Princess- *Ralesia*
Queen of Blue Diamond- Lev
Evil creature- Redy
Brother of Lev- Evy
Sendelia- A village girl
Friend of Sendelia- Rosy
Rabbit- Nautria
Butterfly- Lily
Redy's cat- Robby
King of Switzerland- Leonardo
Grandma of Sendelia- Poppy
Fairy queen- God fairy
Sister of God Fairy- Selfish
Cindrella's Blue Fairy- Mom's Fairy
Son of King Leonardo- Tony
Guard of Blue Diamond Palace- Minet
Son of Redy- Daniel

TWO
START A DAY

Once upon a time in a royal kingdom, there was a young girl with magic eyes. Her eyes were bluish. Looking around, she could turn everything into a lovely and gorgeous place. She was indeed a charming girl. She could do extraordinary things with her eyes. She has a talking butterfly and a rabbit of the exact nature.

Inside her bedroom at about six o'clock on a great summer morning. By that moment, Nautria and Lily entered the room.

Nautria- Ralesia...Ralesia...wake up!

Lily- Oh! Pretty Ralesia, wake up fast!

(Ralesia yawning)

Lily- Good Morning, Ralesia

Nautria- Huh! Finally, you are awake.

Ralesia- Uhh!

(with sleepy eyes and again fall asleep)

Nautria- Oh no! Look Ralesia, your flowers have begun to bloom.

Lily- Sweet fragrant is coming from there. Come on!

Ralesia- Not interested.

(with dizziness)

Kok...Kok..(sound of someone climbing up the stair)

Lily- Ralesia...be quick, Queen Redy is coming.

Redy- Ralesia...Ralesia, open the door.

Nautria- Hurry!!!

Ralesia- C...coming mom. A moment, please.

Redy- Ralesia, what's going on inside?
(opening the door)
Ralesia- Uhhh! Nothing.
Redy- Hmm! What took you so long?
Ralesia- I was just cleaning...
Redy- Is your cleaning more important than me? Didn't you see the time?
Prepare a strawberry cake and a milk tea, wash my clothes, clean my room, stairs, and the door.
Ralesia- But, mom....
Redy- And one more! Bath my Robby.
Ralesia- But, I have to go to bakers...
Redy- I don't want to crack my voice early morning. Shut the door.
(went down. Kok...Kok...)
Ralesia- No time for myself...(weeping)
Nautria- Huh!!!
Lily- I've got an idea....! Let me clean the door with my friends. And Nautria, how about you clean the stair.
Nautria- I can dance at every step. Haha...! What a good brain, bro!
Ralesia- Great, Lily. So I'll prepare the cake and white tea first, then will wash the clothes and take Robby shower. That's going to be great.
Then, they all ran down the stair happily.
Ralesia- Listen! My work is more than you two. So, help me first and I'll be with you later. Today will be a great day. Yeah....!
Nautria- Ah! Lily, we'll have a lot of fun....
Lily- Huh! Finally, I can enjoy the fresh air with both of you.

THREE
ENJOYMENT

In the village, there is a lovely little girl. Her parents died at a young age. She was brought up by her aunt. And she was interested in gardening. She used to sell beautiful bloomy flowers, she went too far places and even took 2/3 days to sell her flowers. While going she used to sing these lines fondly, "Smelly, lovely, sweet flowers. If you buy this, I'll be grateful. She gave in free of cost to children and old people.

On both sides, the enjoyment starts,

Music.....

Royal dress, royal party, garden full of roses along with a little butterfly....

Oh...oh...oh...

Music.....

Lonely, screaming, and wondering with great thought," Is this a life?...full of pain...

Yeh....yeh...yeh...

Music.....

See how t

The princess dance with the prince in her white ball dress.

Oh...oh...oh...

Music......

Royal dress, royal party, garden full of roses along with a little butterfly.....

Oh...oh...oh.....

Music.........

Ralesia finished the preparation of the cake and also washed the Robby. Finally, she entered the garden and play with her magic eyes. Suddenly, the sound of wild rain frightened her and start raining.

Ralesia- Oh! No,

Quick....Lily, Nautria.

Nautria- Ralesia, Lily can't fly.

Ralesia ran towards Lily,

Lily- My feathers get wet. Help! Ra....le...sia...

Nautria- Bring inside, Queen Redy is coming.

FOUR

TRUTH

Queen Redy became so cruel that she began to think about murdering her husband. As the queen wanted to conquer the whole world, killing her husband became her first step.

One day, the king was in a happy mood being his birthday. But the queen was in a frustrated mood. She make a juice mixed with a kind of poison and gave it to the king as a birthday gift. As the king took it happily she began to smile. The king got unconscious after finishing the drink.

Meanwhile, the queen stabs a sword at the king's abdomen. Instantly, the soul of the king turns into a butterfly warning the queen to beware of her coming life. He further said that he'll come back with the princess of "Blue Kingdom". He vanished at a moment. That terrible incident was seen by her son, Daneil. Daneil wept bitterly his body shivering to see his mom in that nature. He promised that he'll take revenge a day.

Five years later, Queen Redy came back with her son and a girl child of ten years namely "Ralesia". The kingdom was unruly till she came back.

On the journey towards her kingdom, Ralesia open the window of the chariot, and a little butterfly came and sat on her nose. It was the same butterfly that the soul turned. She brought it secretly. After reaching the old palace, she explores the palace. Then she saw a little rabbit crying, she sat down and try to touch it but the rabbit got fear and hide behind a bush.

Ralesia- Hello! Little creature, I won't harm you. Can you please come out?

The rabbit slowly came with teary eyes and answer her. Ralesia got confused to hear the sound of talks. Later, she came to know that it was the rabbit who was talking to her. She came to know that rabbit was sad about failing to plant flowers. She promised to help him.

A month later, the area which was filled with bushes was now filled with small growing flowers. They both worked hard a lot. One day,

Nautria- Ralesia, let's stop for today. We've done a lot.

Ralesia- Huh! Just a little bit more.

Suddenly, Ralesia woke up and wonder about what she saw. Then she realized that it was a dream. But still, she got confused.

Ralesia- Is this true? No, no....she is my mom. Calm down....Huh!!!

(sound of twinkling)Then a fairy appears before her and answers her.

Fairy- Yes, my dear. What you saw is the truth.

A long years ago, there is a peaceful kingdom that lived happily by sharing love. They'll prank each other and laugh loudly together. Every day at 8 o'clock, they'll clean the city by singing and dancing. No one in the kingdom felt lonely. This kingdom was known for its wonderful happy life. The kingdom has a blue diamond which is so powerful, that by taking its name from it, the kingdom was known as the "Blue kingdom" of peace.

One day, the king of that kingdom was celebrating his daughter's birthday. The king announced that the heir after his reign will be his daughter so he gifted a birthday gift to her daughter before the villager. The people chorus with joy seeing the equality shown by the king.

The sunray struck the diamond and became so bright that nothing could be seen. And the ray refracted from the diamond goes towards his daughter's eyes. After that, the child's eyes turn blue. The villager got amazed and murmured that it was God's blessing.

And I gave a blessing to the child.

While everyone was enjoying, the evil witch came and destroyed the peace of the kingdom. She demanded the blue diamond from the king, but the king refused. Then when she saw the child, she came to know that the diamond power goes to her. So she demanded the child. As the king again refused, the two got to fight. The king kicked her. In anger, the evil strikes her power to the king. Instantly, The king died. Everyone was shocked to see it and run for their life. She snatch the child from her mother and flew up. She uttered some words to the queen,

"I'll come back for this kingdom. Till then wait for me. And yes don't dream that you'll get your child back".

The witch flies away but the queen runs after her. The queen with rivers of tears in her eyes at last knee down with tiredness and cried a lot. She got changed from that day. She promised to wait for the witch and will fight even with death if comes before. She hardly speaks. The happiness from the village disappeared within a moment. The kingdom got filled with mourn.

The evil witch is the one whom you called mother and for these poor villagers, "Queen Redy" and the little child was you. Ralesia kneels down on the floor and weeps bitterly.

Fairy- Ralesia,

No, don't be upset. Calm down. Be strong. I'll always be by your side, Baby.

Ralesia- But fairy mother, how could I remain silent? She killed my dad.

Fairy- It's all because of the black fairy.

Ralesia- Who is a black fairy?

Fairy- Huh! She is also a fairy like me. She made your father's kingdom turn into a black mysterious place. It was not all the fault of Redy.

Ralesia- You mean, Redy is right.

Fairy- All over she is a devil but indeed another help her.

Ralesia- Black fairy help her to kill my dad?

Fairy- Yes, there was an old black fairy who was kidnapped by Redy. I protect her as much as I could. But I wasn't able to stop Redy. The black fairy was my small sister who has extraordinary power. She was so kind and amazing. But Redy transformed her into an evil fairy. Fairy knows everything about a man's life. So, she told her about Redy. One morning, Redy came with my sister, I try to explain to my sister. But she threw out my hand when I touch her face and said, "Who the hell are you to touch me, bloody hell?" But I cried out, " Siso, I'm your big sis." But she got angry and strike her power to the sky and went away with Redy. My fairy mate tries to console me and some blame me. And Redy tells her to see her future and my sister shows her the next moment of life. And she told Redy the key to grab this world which is the blue diamond. She then locates the place where the blue diamond is found, i.e.the Blue kingdom which was under your father's rule.

Redy sent a message informing that she'll be coming to take the blue diamond officially. Since the next day was your birthday, your parent was upset as they didn't want the villager to know about it and felt sad. So your mother consoles him. The next morning when your birthday got started full of happiness, Redy came and wish you a Happy Birthday. Then she demands the blue diamond. But your father denies it as the villager too refused as all know her real face. So as punishment for not following her words, she killed your father. This was the story and your mother thought that I was the one who was with Redy. So she hates me and I stay away from her but near to you.

Ralesia- God fairy, I want to meet my mom.

Fairy- Not now, my little child. The time will come. Wait for it.

Ralesia- Wait a minute, why didn't I see your sister with Redy?

Fairy- Because she was locked inside a room to prepare poison to destroy those who were against her. (took out a necklace) Take this. Always keep with you and this will help you to reach me. Anytime, you just call me "Good fairy" when you need me.

After saying these few words, she disappeared and Ralesia sat on her bed and weeped inside but she fall asleep without closing the door of her room.

FIVE

SOLVE

The next morning, she woke up to the sound of someone climbing the stair.

(Kok...Kok...)

She jumped down from the bed and hide the necklace given by the God fairy. And Nautria and Lily properly make the bed, but she forgot to make her hair. Redy came entering the room,

Ralesia- Good Morning, mom.

Redy- Hmm! Good Morning....

Ralesia- (remembering the last night incident) Mom, aren't you going to the Blue Kingdom?

Redy- What did you say now? The Blue Kingdom. Ahh! Interesting. But who told you about the Blue Kingdom? Who the hell told you that there is a kingdom known by that name? Tell me now.....

Ralesia- Ah......from Daneil.

Redy- Daniel! Hmm...let me ask him. I didn't sure about your words.

Ralesia- Oh no! What shall I do now? (murmuring)

Redy- Ahmmm...!

Ralesia- Nothing.

Redy- Are you a minister that you'd no time to comb your hair?

Ralesia- I was just cleaning beneath the bed...

Redy- Huh! (make by her magic stick and went to exit)

Ralesia- Huh! Thank you(whispering)

Redy- (cleaning throat) Ahem..!

Ralesia- (to Lily) You helped me.

Robby- Grrrr! (roaring)

Ralesia hides the butterfly and says,

Ralesia- Anything remains, Mr.

Robby ran after Redy to the exit. In the village, Sendelia was in a happy mood.

Sendelia- Hmm! La...la...la...

Rosy(a lady who is fond of love) came,

Rosy- A very good morning, Sendelia, my sweet lady.

Sendelia- Ahh! Rosy, A very pleasant morning. Please have a sit.

She gave Rosy a rose and said,

Sendelia- For you.

Rosy- Oh that's so romantic. Thank you.

Sendelia- So I know that you are eager to tell me about yesterday's date.

Rosy- No...no...no....!!!(shout)

Everyone around them stares at her.

Sendelia- R...o...s...y....!

Rosy- I wasn't pleased with him. I didn't. I look charming and enormous, didn't I? Is everything all right? Why everyone is staring at me?

Sendelia- Ahh! Seems like you look more beautiful today.

Suddenly, Redy arrived. Everyone ran inside their houses and shut their doors. Then, Redy cried out,

Redy- Sendelia, Where is my flower? It's your last chance. Give me back now....

Sendelia- Never! You know that I can't live without it.

Redy got angry and destroyed all her flowers with her stick.

Redy- Get lost, I'll give you five more days or else.... I hope you knew the consequences.

Sendelia- No...my flowers. Stop, please....(weeping)

Redy- (shouting angrily) Didn't you know that I'm the queen of this world, no one can stop me. You, little bustard(beat the horse and ride away).

Sendelia- She left me nothing not even a single flower....

Rosy- (touch her shoulder) Huh!

Sendelia- She came from nowhere and crush my life again.

Sendelia's aunt came and saw the flowers, she exclaimed,

Aunt- Oh my God! The flowers...Sendelia, what happens?

Sendelia rushed towards and hug her.

Aunt- Ahh! My child. No...no...Who makes my child cry? Rosy...why is she crying?

Rosy- She came again and destroyed all the flowers and warned Sendelia to give the flower in five days.

Aunt- How dare she! Hmm! This time too she escape from me. Rosy help me in cleaning these.

Sendelia- No... It's my fault so I'll clean it. And I won't sell flowers from today.

Aunt- Sendelia, why are you punishing yourself when the mistake was her not you? Be strong, my dear. (hug her)

Three hours later,

Aunt- Sendelia...Sendelia...

Entering her room and saw Sendelia weeping aside and she uttered some words,

"Huh! I'm sorry, dear. I'm not perfect to be your aunt. I can't make my only child smile."

Sendelia- Poppy Aunt, you're the only one who is for me. I love you.

Aunt- I love you too, dear. (kiss on her forehead) Ahh! Today you're shining more than your golden flower. (they both laugh) So do you know what special I prepare for you today? Can you guess?

Sendelia- Really? My mouth is watering....what would it be?

Aunt- (laughing) Haha...okay...okay...

After dinner, Sendelia fall asleep at the table where her golden flower was kept. Poppy Aunt entered the room and saw her,

Aunt- Huh! My poor child. Sendelia...(in a low voice) everything's gonna be okay. No one can take your flower from you. Now get to sleep in your bed.

She kisses her and went out after she slept.

Aunt- It's hard to guess what would be her next phase of life.

She then wore her overcoat and ride her house towards a cave. She entered the cave and whisper some words. Then God fairy came with a sound of twinkling.

Aunt- Greetings!

Fairy- Why did you call me?

Aunt- I hope you're well and fine these days.

Fairy- Nothing serious. Go on with your topic.

Aunt- My child got in trouble again.

Fairy- Oh my Sendelia! What happens to her?

Poppy narrates the incident to her with tears.

Fairy- Ah! Mon Dieu...

Aunt- I didn't know what to do.

Fairy- The two children had enough of her. My Ralesia and Sendelia...

Aunt- Is Ralesia still in her cage?

Fairy- Yes....

Aunt- She is a woman. She must think about the mother living without her child.

Fairy- Don't take her as a woman she is a devil.

Aunt- But fairy my child remains crying from dusk. What should I do now?

Fairy- Don't worry. I think tomorrow is her birthday. So go and decorate so that she could forget all and be happy.

Aunt- Let me try. Good to see you. Bye.

Fairy- My blessing is with you all.

God fairy disappeared after that and Poppy returned and make the house beautiful as she could. And she makes a cake of vanilla flavor which is Sendelia's favorite. Sendelia woke up in the morning and saw the surprise which she was shocked to see it. Then Poppy and Rosy came singing from behind,

Aunt- The sun shines bright in the sky. The birds sing sweet flying around. The flower is blooming greatly.

Rosy- They seem like wishing her....

Chorus- Happy Birthday to you....Dear Sendelia.

SIX

GETTING WEAK

Redy came to Selfish's room. She was so angry with Sendelia that she even wanted to kill her.

Redy- (shouts) Sendelia, you'll be dying on my hand soon.

Selfish- Oh dear, the child plays you very nicely.

Selfish gave a smile to Redy after saying that. Then, Redy stare at her angrily and said,

Redy- What do you think of me? That I'll let her go easily. Do your work. Make me the queen of this universe now......

Selfish- Just like you say, you can't grab this world so easily.

Redy- Just shut up. Don't turn me up or else you know what I'll do to you?

Selfish pour water into a glass and give it to Redy.

Selfish- Let your brain rest for a while. Drink it.

Redy threw the glass.

Selfish- Calm down, my dear. Everything will be yours. Be patient.

Then, she brings out a diamond and said,

Selfish- Blue Diamond. Hmm....!

On the other side, when Lev was looking outside standing at the barrister, she suddenly got her visual uncleared and fall unconscious. Then the guards rushed in and rang the alarm bill. Immediately the doctor arrived and checked her health and said that she is too weak and she needs to be happy and not think much.

Evy then came out following the doctor and asked about her condition,

Evy-Doctor! What was that?

Doctor-It's a heart attack, but don't worry, sir. Please let her take the medicine in time.

Evy-Thanks you.

Mom's fairy appeared instantly and cried out,

Mom's fairy-Oh my poor lady! What's all this?

She then touches her hand. She slowly open her eyes and said,

Lev-Ralesia!

Mom's fairy-Lev, are you alright? Here, drinks this water. It'll help you, dear.

She flew around and tell Evy that she was getting weak day by day as her power gets to lose. Ralesia can only save her. Then Evy sat down near Lev and hold her hand and said,

Evy- Are you feeling easy now? I'm sorry that I was not with you.

Lev- It's okay, my boy. See, I'm fantastic well.

Evy hug her sister while Mom's fairy was in great tense about Lev. She murmured within,

Mom's fairy- Oh God! What was their fault that you give them such a painful life?

On the other side, Ralesia became so worried and walked up and down the room. Nautria then breaks the silence,

Nautria- Ralesia, stop thinking much. We'll find out a way to make it all right.

Lily- Yes, Ralesia, just take it easy.

Ralesia- Something isn't alright. And it's troubling me.

Lily- Why didn't you ask for your necklace?

Nautria- Aha! That's awesome. Come on, Ralesia.

Ralesia- What a brilliant idea!

Raetia then took out her necklace and said,

Ralesia-Show me, my mother.

Then Lev Appeared on her necklace lying on her bed with closed eyes. Ralesia then weep to see it and asked,

Ralesia-Mom, what happen to you?

Lily-Ralesia!......

Nutria-She might be taking rest.

God fairy then appeared on her necklace and asked,

God fairy -Ralesia do you hear me?

Ralesia- God fairy! What's going on? What happened to my mom?

God fairy- I know you'll ask me the same. Now listen to me carefully, your

Mother is sick. Only a few hours had left for her in this world. Her power is losing.

Ralesia- No...no...! She can't leave me easily. I'll never let her go.

God fairy- Save her. Come quick.

God fairy show the way to reach the palace and ordered her to be quick as the way is somehow far from their area. Ralesia wore her overcoat and put the necklace inside her pocket.

Nautria- I'll come with you, Ralesia.

Lily- Yes, me too.

Ralesia- Okay. So, you two need to help me.

SEVEN

CAUGHT BACK

They ran towards her door and when Ralesia opened it, she strikes with Daniel. Then Daniel shout as Ralesia was wholly covered.

Ralesia- Shhhh! It's me, Ralesia.

Daniel- Whow...! What are you doing with all this stuff? Where are you rushing?

Ralesia- Daniel, let me tell you later. Now please let me get out of this house.

Daniel- Okay...!!! Follow me.

They came down from the window with rope and heard someone riding a horse towards them. They got escaped and reached the market. Daniel ran to buy some food for their journey but on his return, he strikes with Sendelia and her flowers fall off above them. The two fell to the ground. Sendelia sit up by rubbing her forehead and said,

Sendelia- Can't you see the way?

Daniel- I'm so sorry. Are you alright?

Sendelia- Ya...I'm fine.

Daniel- Oh no! Rales sis....

He then ran away leaving her with all the flowers on the ground.

Sendelia- Hey! Pick up these flowers...

Daniel- I'm sorry!!!

When he reaches there, he finds Ralesia at Redy's hand. Then Redy brought them back home full of anger and start to question them,

Redy- Did you think that I'm a fool?

Daniel- Mom....!

Redy- (shouts) Shut up your mouth.

Daniel then stared at the floor. And Redy pointed toward Ralesia and said,

Redy- You...being a sister, you taught him to go out of the house.

Daniel- Mom, that's....

Redy- Did I ask you anything? Go and get to your room. I'll come to see you later.

Daniel- But...

Redy- Don't make me repeat. I said go...

Daniel exits the room by looking at her sis. Redy then shut the door and came near Ralesia and start to sob,

Redy- Oh my child! I'm sorry that I shout at you. I'm sorry.... sorry.

Ralesia- No, it's all my fault. I shouldn't take Daniel out.

Redy- Hahaha.... (laugh) And you think that you can go out.

Ralesia- Why couldn't I? Am I born to be only at home?

Redy- You speak before me. What didn't I assure you that you want to get out?

Ralesia- Really? Did you didn't know that my mom is dying because of you?

Redy- Mother, who is your mother? Did you have another one rather than mine?

Ralesia- Then promise me that I'm your child.

Redy- Did you think of life as a drama?

Ralesia- Then why did you kill my dad? Why are you troubling my mom and me?

Redy- Do you want to know the reason? Because he didn't obey my words. He didn't obey the words of Queen Redy who is the ruler of this world.

Redy then started to sing,

"No one,

There is no one who can defeat me,

Coz I'm the one, the only one...

La....la....la...
La...la...la...
La...la...la...
Yes, that is me,
The queen Redy....
The queen of this world...
The queen of this whole universe....
The owner of Blue...DIAMOND,
It belongs to me...
To Redy....
Oh! I must first grab that blue diamond,
And the world is waiting for me...
To wear that crown....
I need it,
The golden flower...
I need it...

She then pulls up Ralesia's room and makes it a tall tower and covered her room with magical green glass which has a high reflection. She then sang further,

Yes, I killed him...
He loved me,
But I had him as he was the king...
Oh....my sweetheart...
My darling...
I just remove him
Out of my way....
So, no one could stop me
No one..!
'Coz I'm the queen......

EIGHT

ESCAPE

Redy then went away by locking the door and Ralesia get locked inside. She cried out,

Ralesia- Hey! Let me get out of here. Hey...!

She then fell to her knees and sobbed,

Ralesia- I'm sorry...Mom.... sorry.

But after Redy went away, Daniel came up the stair rushing and try to enter but he was thrown out by the glass. Ralesia then screamed out,

Ralesia- Daniel, watch out...

Daniel- Ahh! Are you okay, Rales? I'm fine.

Ralesia- Huh! Daniel, let me tell you the truth. My mom is dying and she needs me. Please do something and take me out of here.

Daniel- Okay, let me try.

He then kicks the glass but he was again thrown away with high force. This time his lips got hurt and start to bleed. Ralesia then screamed out,

Ralesia- Daniel.....! Did you get hurt?

Daniel- ...Ya...I'm okay.

Ralesia- What will I do now? Mom...I'm sorry, I have no way...(weep)

Nautria- Ralesia... (in a low voice) Stop crying.

Lily- Ralesia, I'm sorry that we can't help you out today.

They all stare down sadly. But a teardrop of Ralesia falls. Instantly, a bright light came from her eyes, and the cover got disappeared. All got amazed to see it,

Nautria- Wowww....

Lily- It's amazing.

Daniel- Rales...! Am I dreaming?

Ralesia closed her eyes and touched and smile with tears. Then they all ran down from her room. Sendelia came with her flowers but when she saw someone come by riding a horse at a far distance, she hides behind the bushes by uttering some words.

Sendelia- Did she know my way?...

Redy then pas her within a second as she rides so fast that Sendelia can't see her but heard only the horse-riding sound. She then came out and sighed,

Sendelia- Maybe this way led to her home. I can find some clues if I went there.

She then walked as quickly as she can until she saw a black house-like palace filled with full of scrapers. She started to sing,

Sendelia- Smelly, lovely, sweet flowers. If you kindly buy one then I'll offer you another one.

She then entered the palace and she started to fear seeing the darkness inside and said,

Sendelia- Hello! Is anyone here?

But she could only hear the echo of her voice. Robby came from a dark corner and come towards her.

Robby- roar....

Sendelia- Hey! Su...Su...Get away...Su...Hey, leave my skirt...

Daniel and Ralesia came running down the stair and saw her. Daniel came rushing and kicked Robby. Robby started to crawl angrily.

Robby- Miao...!

Daniel- Hey, what are you doing here? And I'm sorry for that.

Sendelia- You!!! Let me ask you why you are here.

Daniel- Come on. This is my house.

Sendelia- What! Are you kidding me? I know you two exactly. What did you take away from here? This is Redy's palace. I won't spare you both.

Daniel stared at Ralesia amusedly and said,

Daniel- Did you address a person like that at your first meeting?

Ralesia- Stop, both of you. He is the son of Redy and I'm her sister. Please stop fighting. I'm in a hurry. And follow us this is not a good place.

They ran away which led to the way of Blue Kingdom. Redy reached Sendelia's home there and shouted her name.

Redy- Sendelia........ you can't hide anymore, come out.

Redy then entered the house and saw Rosy and Poppy,

Redy- Rosy, where is Sendelia?

Poppy- Huh...! That's good to hear.

Redy- Did you wanna die in my head?

Poppy- Who said that the victory is for the villain? The hero always wins.

Redy- Just shut up. You, old bitch. Rosy....!

Rosy was sweating when she took her name and response in a trembling voice,

Rosy- I don't know, your highness.

Redy- Then what else did you know?

Poppy- Life still amazes me why the villains always remain strange. Poor Queen, she left with her golden flower in the early morning.

Redy- Enough!Yaaaa....

Redy strikes her power and within a second all the humans and the objects in the village turn into statues of how they were. She got disappeared and returned home. Robby came running towards her and started to crawl. She saw Robby's head swell. Redy was shocked to see it.

Redy- Oh my! Who the hell did this to you?

NINE
MISERIES

On the way of Ralesia, Nautria and Lily came running and screamed out so that she can hear.

Nautria- Ralesia... wait for me. Wait.

Lily- Ralesia...

Ralesia- Come on...Be quick.

Nautria- But where are we going?

Ralesia- To our kingdom.

Nautria- Our kingdom?

They got stuck in a forest after a long run as they got confused seeing the four different ways. Ralesia then took out her necklace and call the fairy.

Ralesia- God fairy! Which way should I follow? It's showing us four ways.

God fairy- Oh my child! Come soon. Follow the second one. I'll be there for you. Sit on this flying carpet, this will help you come fast.

God fairy then gave her a flying carpet and disappeared from the necklace. Ralesia put her necklace inside and asked,

Ralesia- So guys, are you all ready?

Chorus- Yes.

Ralesia- Then here we go.

Then the carpet started to fly up. Robby tells all the incidents to Redy at the palace. Redy then laughed,

Redy- My Robby, they can't reach so easily.

Then she remembered when she divided the way into four ways in the forest upon her return. Then Redy stood before her magic ball and ordered,

Redy- Show me my Ralesia...ha...ha..ha..

The children appeared flying on the carpet at the ball. Redy was shocked to see it. So, she shouts angrily,

Redy- Selfish.... now...

Selfish appeared instantly at her flying horse. She smiled and said,

Selfish- I know you'll call me. Don't worry, dear. There is another misery left to face by them. And that won't be so easy.

Then the two vanished with Robby. There in the Blue kingdom, Lev got very serious and she was whispering only her daughter's name. Evy got worried and asked Mom's fairy.

Evy- You are the one who knows everything. Please tell me whether she'll come or not.

Mom's fairy- My son, she'll come surely...

Evy- But when my sister is dying....

On the Ralesia's way, they met a dangerous place where the ground was cracked and the fire was burning inside the crack holes. The trees were dry with no leaves.

Nautria- Hey, why my butt is feeling warm. Ahh! It's comforting me after a long journey in cold air.

He then looked down but he fell all of a sudden and he cried out,

Nautria- Ahhhh...! Ralesia....!

Ralesia- Nautria, carpet fly down.

But the carpet didn't move.

"Fly down!"

Still, the carpet tail show as she's refusing.

"Please, you can do it."

Then the carpet starts to move slowly.

"Everyone ready. Now go..."

They flew down but Sendelia shouts and grabs Daniel's hand in fear. But her nails pinned daniel's hand as he got hurt, and he started to scream. Nautria was stuck in between a tree branch. He closes his eyes and prays. Ralesia pick him up and kept in her lap. But still, his eyes were closed and his body was shaking in fear. Then everyone laughed at his cute nature. He opens his left eye and when he saw Ralesia, he hugged her tightly and said,

Nautria- Ahh! Ralesia, I thought that I wouldn't be alive and see you again.

They all laughed. Lily came and sat at his ear. Then Ralesia open her eyes and let all the fire turn into water and the tree began to bloom within a second. Sendelia was shocked and asked Daniel,

Sendelia- Is this your sister?

Ralesia- I won't confuse you more. I'm the princess of Blue Diamond and my eyes had the power of blue diamond which Queen Redy needed the most to become the queen of this universe. So, she snatches me from my mom when I was only 10 years old. She also killed my father. Our family had magical power and we lived by it. Now my mom is losing her power. She needs me.

Sendelia- I think that it was only me that she's troubling but you too.

Ralesia- What happens to you?

Sendelia- I have a golden flower which my parents gifted me as I love flowers. It is a magical flower, you can turn the whole world into a garden with that. I live by selling flowers with the help of that. And Redy wants it from me.

Daniel- Huh! I'm so sorry to both of you.

Ralesia- Daniel, why did you say that? You are not like her even though she is your mother but she's a bitch. You are my little good brother.

TEN

LATE

Nautria- Ralesia, look at that.

They saw a beautiful palace ahead. They stare with their mouth open in amusement. Lily exclaimed,

Lily- Wow!!! It's beautiful.

When they look down, they saw the villagers before the palace in silence. Ralesia started to get more worried. Then they saw a room that was surrounded by guards.

Sendelia- It must be her mom. What will we do now? Princess.

Nautria- Ha..ha.. Let me handle it.

Ralesia saw her mother lying on the bed. Her tears started to fall. She tried to enter, but the guards stopped her,

Minet- Hey! You can't enter the queen's room like that. Who are you?

Daniel- What are you talking about? Man, how are you? Ah, such a long time.

Daniel then hugs the guard and lets Ralesia enter the room. He acts as if he were his friend. Tony is the son of King Leonardo, which is the ruler of the Swiz kingdom who comes to meet the queen. He remains to guard the queen as he knows Redy. He is a good friend of Minet. Daniel then took Minet away. Sendelia then acts as unconscious and fell on Tony. So, Tony let her sit and call for water. But Lily sat on Tony's nose,

Tony- Hey, su..su...

Then Tony run away with lily sitting at his nose. Sendelia entered the room. Ralesia ran and hugged her mother.

Mom's fairy- You've grown up soon. My child.

Lev- Ahh! Ralesia.

The two wept by hugging but Lev's hand falls at that moment. When Ralesia releases and looks at her, she found her dead. Ralesia then holds her hand and cries bitterly. Her tears fall on Lev's face.

Mom's fairy- You've come a little late....

Ralesia- I'm sorry...

But Lev's hand began to move and hold ralesia's hand. She got amazed and cry out,

Ralesia- Mom...

Evy- Sister.

Lev then rose and hug her child. Daniel came rushing with Tony and Minet. Mom's fairy laughs and says,

Mom's fairy- She got alive again. This is wonderful.

At that moment, Queen Redy and Selfish came entering from the window with their flying horse.

Redy- Ah Lev! You got alive again to make me kill you. I'll miss you, dear. Ya...

She then strikes the power to Lev. Ralesia then stood before her mother and the power strikes into her.

Ralesia- No....

The power enters her body and the whole sky turns dark. All the blue colors disappeared. Lev then shout,

Lev- Ralesia....

Redy- Huh! Ralesia...

Mom's fairy- Don't dare to take her name!

Lev hugs her child like a mad woman. Evy holds her.

Evy- Sister...

Daniel- Rales sister.

Nautria- Ralesia....

All rushed and sat beside her. But as Mom's fairy said,

Mom's fairy- Let's show her respect. May she be in God's place.

All the knees are down on the floor and remain silent except Lev. Lev then closes her eyes and touches Ralesia's face. After a while, Ralesia's face began to glow and flew up and a bright light got exposed her and turned into a beautiful princess dressed in blue and a crown on her forehead. Everyone got shocked. Redy then started to miss herself,

Redy- No...no...No......

She shouts and turned into a rat. Robby ran to catch after her while all the statues in the village turned to their lives again and the blue sky appeared again with all blue things. Lily turned to human again and hug Daniel. God fairy then appears in the room and hugs Selfish.

Daniel- Dad!!!

Selfish- Sister....

ELEVEN

TO NORMAL

Meanwhile, all the villagers of Redy's kingdom approached there and have a grand celebration. The two fairies went to their fairyland while Nautria lived with Ralesia as she makes a small palace for the two and a cute garden for Nautria. Daniel returns with his dad to their kingdom and lives happily. People enjoyed. Rosy came rushing and hug Sendelia and exclaimed,

Rosy- He accepts me! I did it...

She then screamed out. Everyone stares at her like before. She then laughed out with Sendelia. Sendelia got married to Daniel. They lived happily.

And the story finishes like this.", an old woman said and closed the book. A little two children exclaimed,

"Wow! I wish I had magic like Princess Ralesia!"

"Haha...It's all about the story."

"But what if I had, Grandma!"

The old lady then laughed and kept the book in her cupboard and locked it and put the key inside her apron pocket. Then she holds the hands of the two children and came towards the bed. She makes the two sleep in their beds. Then she sat down at her fireplace and took out a photo of Princess Ralesia with a girl child and Prince Tony and smiled. She then uttered some words,

"The time went so soon; I miss you mom."

Moral

"There are still several children who are motherless and praying every single moment for a mother. So love your mother, give all the affection as nothing is more than a mother".

Dear mom,

(L) Mrs.Fatima

"REST IN PEACE"